A
Christmas
Carol

A Christmas Carol

by Charles Dickens

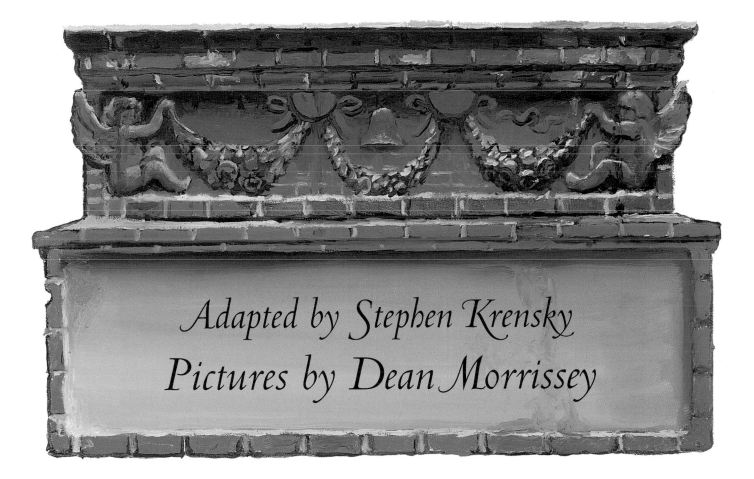

Adapted by Stephen Krensky
Pictures by Dean Morrissey

HarperCollins Publishers

A Christmas Carol
Copyright © 2001 by Dean Morrissey
Manufactured in China by South China Printing Company Ltd.
All rights reserved.
www.harperchildrens.com

Library of Congress Cataloging-in-Publication Data
Krensky, Stephen.
A Christmas carol / adapted by Stephen Krensky ;
pictures by Dean Morrissey.
p.   cm.
Summary: A miser learns the true meaning of Christmas when three
ghostly visitors review his past and foretell his future.
ISBN 0-06-028577-X – ISBN 0-06-443606-3 (pbk.)
[1. Christmas–Fiction.   2. Ghosts–Fiction.   3. England–Fiction.]
I. Morrissey, Dean, ill.   II. Dickens, Charles, 1812–1870.   Christmas
carol.   III. Title.
PZ7.K883 Cf 2001   [Fic]–dc21   00-040885   CIP   AC

❖

For Phyllis Wender

STAVES

A
Christmas
Carol

MARLEY'S GHOST

Marley was dead, to begin with. There is no doubt whatever about that. The register of his burial was signed by the clergyman, the clerk, and the undertaker. Old Marley was as dead as a doornail.

Did Scrooge know he was dead? Of course he did. Scrooge had been his partner for I don't know how many years. He was Marley's sole executor, his sole administrator, his sole friend, and sole mourner.

Scrooge never even painted out Old Marley's name. There it stood, years afterward, above the warehouse door: Scrooge and Marley. Oh! but Scrooge was a tight-fisted hand at the grindstone—a squeezing, wrenching, grasping, scraping, clutching, covetous, old sinner!

Once upon a time—of all the good days in the year, on Christmas Eve—old Scrooge sat busy in his countinghouse. It was cold, bleak, biting weather. The fog poured in at every chink and keyhole.

The door of Scrooge's office was open that he might keep a watchful eye on his clerk, Bob Cratchit, who was copying letters in a dismal little cell beyond.

"A merry Christmas, Uncle!" cried a cheerful voice from the doorway.

"Bah!" said Scrooge. "Humbug!"

It was Scrooge's nephew, who had so heated himself walking that he was all in a glow.

"Christmas a humbug, Uncle! You don't mean that?"

"I do," said Scrooge. "Merry Christmas! What right have you to be merry? You're poor enough."

"Come, then," returned the nephew. "What right have you to be dismal? You're rich enough."

Scrooge, having no better answer, said "Bah!" again; and followed it up with "Humbug."

"Don't be cross, Uncle!"

"What else can I be? What's Christmas to you but a time for finding yourself a year older, but not an hour richer? If I could work my will, every idiot who says 'Merry Christmas' should be boiled with his own pudding, and buried with a stake of holly through his heart."

"Don't be angry, Uncle. Come! Dine with us tomorrow."

"Good afternoon," said Scrooge.

"I am sorry, with all my heart, to find you so resolute. Still, A Merry Christmas, Uncle!"

"Good afternoon!" said Scrooge.

"And A Happy New Year!"

Scrooge's nephew left the room without an angry word. The clerk, as he let the nephew out, let two other gentlemen in.

"Scrooge and Marley's, I believe," said one of them. "Have I the pleasure of addressing Mr. Scrooge or Mr. Marley?"

"Mr. Marley has been dead these seven years," Scrooge replied. "He died seven years ago, this very night."

"We have no doubt," said the gentleman, "that his generosity is well represented by his surviving partner."

Scrooge frowned.

"At this festive season, Mr. Scrooge," the gentleman continued, "we try to make some provision for the Poor."

"Are there no prisons?" asked Scrooge.

"Plenty of prisons," said the gentleman.

"And workhouses?" demanded Scrooge. "Are they still in operation?"

"They are," returned the gentleman.

"Oh!" said Scrooge. "I was afraid, from what you said, that something had occurred to stop them."

"Nevertheless," returned the gentleman, "a few of us endeavor to raise a fund to buy the Poor some meat and drink. What shall I put you down for?"

"Nothing!" Scrooge replied. "I don't make merry at Christmas, and I can't afford to make idle people merry. I support the places I have mentioned. Those who are badly off must go there."

"Many can't go there; and many would rather die."

"If they would rather die," said Scrooge, "they had better do it, and decrease the surplus population. Good afternoon!"

Seeing clearly that their interview was over, the gentlemen withdrew.

At length the hour of closing arrived. With an ill will Scrooge admitted the fact to the expectant clerk, who instantly snuffed his candle out.

"You'll want all day tomorrow, I suppose?" said Scrooge.

The clerk observed that it was only once a year.

"A poor excuse for picking a man's pocket every twenty-fifth of December!" said Scrooge. "But I suppose you must have the whole day. Be here all the earlier next morning."

The office was closed in a twinkling, and Scrooge walked out with a growl.

He took his melancholy dinner in his usual melancholy tavern; and having read all the newspapers and reviewed his bankbook, he went home to bed.

Now, it is a fact that there was nothing at all particular about the knocker on Scrooge's door. Scrooge had seen it, night and morning, the whole of the time he had lived there. And yet Scrooge, having his key in the lock, suddenly saw—not a knocker, but Marley's face.

Marley's face. It was not angry or ferocious, but looked simply as Marley used to look. The hair was curiously stirred, as if by breath or hot air; and, though the eyes were open, they were perfectly motionless.

As Scrooge looked fixedly at this phenomenon, it was a knocker again. To say that he was not startled would be untrue. But he put his hand upon the key, turned it sturdily, walked in, and lighted his candle.

He *did* pause before shutting the door; and he *did* look cautiously behind it. But there was nothing on the back of the door, except the screws and nuts that held the knocker on, so he said "Pooh, pooh!" and closed it with a bang.

The sound traveled through the house like thunder. But Scrooge was not a man to be frightened by echoes. He walked across the hall and up the stairs, trimming his candle as he went.

Sitting room, bedroom, storeroom. All were as they should be.

Nobody under the table, nobody under the sofa. Nobody under the bed, nobody in the closet. Quite satisfied, Scrooge closed his door and double-locked himself in. Thus secured against surprise, he put on his dressing gown, slippers, and nightcap, and sat down before the fire to take his gruel.

As he sat back in the chair, his glance rested upon a disused bell that hung in the room. As he looked, he saw this bell begin to swing. It swung softly at first; but soon it rang out loudly; and so did every bell in the house.

The bells ceased as they had begun, together. They were succeeded by a clanking noise, deep down below.

The cellar door flew open with a booming sound, and then Scrooge heard the noise much louder, on the floors below; then coming up the stairs; then coming straight toward his door.

"It's humbug still!" he said. "I won't believe it."

His color changed though, when, without a pause, it came on through the heavy door, and passed into the room.

The same face: the very same. Marley stood before him in his pigtail, waistcoat, tights, and boots. The chain he carried was clasped about his middle. It wound about him like a tail; and it was made of cashboxes, keys, padlocks, ledgers, and heavy purses wrought in steel.

Though Scrooge looked the phantom through and through, he was still incredulous.

11

"How now!" said Scrooge. "What do you want with me?"

"Much!" Marley's voice, no doubt about it.

"Who are you?" Scrooge demanded.

"In life I was your partner, Jacob Marley."

"Can you—can you sit down?" asked Scrooge doubtfully.

"I can."

"Do it, then."

The Ghost sat down on the opposite side of the fireplace. "You don't believe in me," he observed.

"I don't," said Scrooge.

"Why do you doubt your senses?"

"Because," said Scrooge, "a little thing affects them. A slight disorder of the stomach makes them cheats. You may be an undigested bit of beef, a blot of mustard, a crumb of cheese, a fragment of an underdone potato. There's more of gravy than of grave about you, whatever you are!"

At this, the spirit raised a frightful cry and shook its chain. Scrooge fell upon his knees and clasped his hands before his face.

"Mercy!" he said. "Dreadful apparition, why do you trouble me?"

"Man of the worldly mind!" replied the Ghost, "do you believe in me or not?"

"I do," said Scrooge. "I must. But why do spirits walk the earth, and why do they come to me?"

"It is required of every man," the Ghost returned, "that the spirit within him should walk abroad among his fellow-men. If that spirit goes not forth in life, it is condemned to do so after death."

"You are fettered," said Scrooge, trembling. "Tell me why?"

"I wear the chain I forged in life," replied the Ghost. "I made it link by link, and yard by yard."

Scrooge trembled more and more.

"Would you know," pursued the Ghost, "the weight and length of the strong coil you bear yourself? It was full as heavy and as long as this, seven Christmas Eves ago. You have labored mightily on it since."

Scrooge glanced about, expecting to find himself surrounded by some fifty or sixty fathoms of iron cable. But he could see nothing.

"Jacob," he said imploringly. "Old Jacob Marley, tell me more. Speak comfort to me, Jacob!"

"I have none to give," the Ghost replied. "Nor can I tell you what I would like to. A very little more is permitted to me. I cannot rest, I cannot stay, I cannot linger anywhere."

"But you were always a good man of business, Jacob," faltered Scrooge.

"Business!" cried the Ghost, wringing its hands again. "Mankind was my business. The common welfare was my business. Charity, mercy, forbearance, and benevolence were all my business!"

It held up its chain at arm's length and flung it heavily upon the ground again.

"Hear me!" cried the Ghost. "My time is nearly gone. I am here

tonight to warn you, that you have yet a chance of escaping my fate. A chance and hope of my procuring, Ebenezer."

"You were always a good friend to me," said Scrooge. "Thank you!"

"You will be haunted," resumed the Ghost, "by Three Spirits."

Scrooge's countenance fell. "I—I think I'd rather not," he said.

"Without their visits," said the Ghost, "you cannot hope to shun the path I tread. Look to see me no more; and for your own sake, remember what has passed between us!"

The apparition then began walking backward from Scrooge. At every step it took, the window raised itself a little, so that when the specter reached it, it was wide open. The specter, after listening for a moment, floated out upon the bleak, dark night.

Scrooge followed to the window, desperate in his curiosity. He looked out.

The air was filled with phantoms, wandering in restless haste, and moaning as they went. Every one of them wore chains like Marley's Ghost.

Whether these creatures faded into mist, or mist enshrouded them, he could not tell. But they and their spirit voices faded together.

Scrooge closed the window and examined the door by which the Ghost had entered. It was still double-locked, and the bolts were undisturbed. He tried to say "Humbug!" but stopped at the first syllable. Much in need of repose, he went straight to bed and fell asleep at once.

15

THE FIRST OF THE THREE SPIRITS

When Scrooge awoke, it was so dark that he could scarcely distinguish the transparent window from the opaque walls of his chamber. The chimes of a neighboring church struck the four quarters, and Scrooge listened for the hour. As the deep, hollow bell sounded midnight, light flashed up in the room, and the curtains of his bed were drawn.

Scrooge, starting up, found himself face to face with an unearthly visitor.

It was a strange figure—like a child, yet like an old man diminished to a child's proportions. Its hair was white as if with age, and yet the face had not a wrinkle. From the crown of its head there sprung a bright clear jet of light, and it wore a great extinguisher for a cap.

"Are you the Spirit, sir, whose coming was foretold to me?" asked Scrooge.

"I am." The voice was soft and gentle.

"Who and what are you?" Scrooge demanded.

"I am the Ghost of Christmas Past."

"Long past?" inquired Scrooge.

"No. Your past."

Scrooge then made bold to inquire what business brought him there.

"Your welfare," said the Ghost.

It put out its strong hand and clasped him gently by the arm.

"Rise! And walk with me."

The grasp, though gentle, was not to be resisted. Scrooge rose. They passed through the wall, and stood upon an open country road. The city had entirely vanished.

"Good Heaven!" said Scrooge, clasping his hands together. "I was bred in this place. I was a boy here!"

"You recollect the way?" inquired the Spirit.

"Remember it!" cried Scrooge with fervor. "I could walk it blindfold."

They walked along the road, Scrooge recognizing every gate, and post, and tree. Some shaggy ponies now were seen trotting toward them with boys upon their backs, who called to other boys in country gigs and carts.

"These are but shadows of the things that have been," said the Ghost. "They have no awareness of us."

The travelers came on; and as they came, Scrooge knew and named them every one. He heard them give each other Merry Christmas as they parted for their homes.

"The school is not quite deserted," said the Ghost. "A solitary child is left there still."

Scrooge said he knew it. And he sobbed.

They left the high road and approached a mansion of dull red brick. It was a large house, but one of broken fortunes. The spacious offices were little used, their walls damp and mossy, their windows broken.

They went, the Ghost and Scrooge, to a long, bare room. A lonely boy was reading near a feeble fire; and Scrooge wept to see his poor forgotten self as he used to be.

"I wish," Scrooge muttered, putting his hand in his pocket after drying his eyes with his cuff.

"What is the matter?" asked the Ghost.

"There was a boy singing a Christmas Carol at my door last night. I should like to have given him something—that's all."

The Ghost smiled thoughtfully and waved its hand. "Let us see another Christmas!"

Scrooge's former self grew larger at the words, and the room became a little darker and more dirty. The panels shrunk, the windows cracked, and fragments of plaster fell out of the ceiling.

The door opened. A little girl came darting in and

19

put her arms about the boy's neck.

"I have come to bring you home, dear brother!" said the child, clapping her tiny hands.

"Home, little Fan?" returned the boy.

"Yes!" said the child. "Home, for ever and ever. Father is so much kinder than he used to be. He spoke so gently to me one dear night, that I was not afraid to ask him once more if you might come home; and he said, Yes, you should, and sent me in a coach to bring you."

She clapped her hands and laughed.

"Always a delicate creature," said the Ghost. "But she had a large heart!"

"So she had," cried Scrooge.

"She died a woman," said the Ghost, "and had, as I think, children."

"One child," Scrooge returned.

"True," said the Ghost. "Your nephew!"

Scrooge seemed uneasy and answered briefly, "Yes."

Although they had only just left the school behind them, they were now in the busy thoroughfares of a city. Here too it was Christmastime again, but it was evening, and the streets were lighted up.

The Ghost stopped at a warehouse door and asked Scrooge if he knew it.

"Know it!" said Scrooge. "I was apprenticed here!"

They went in. At the sight of an old gentleman sitting behind a high desk, Scrooge cried in great excitement:

"Why, it's old Fezziwig! Bless his heart; it's Fezziwig alive again!"

Old Fezziwig laid down his pen and looked up at the clock, which pointed to the hour of seven. He rubbed his hands, adjusted his capacious waistcoat, and called out in a comfortable, rich, jovial voice:

"Yo ho, there! Ebenezer! Dick!"

Scrooge's former self, now grown a young man, came briskly in, accompanied by his fellow prentice.

"Yo ho, my boys!" said Fezziwig. "No more work tonight. Christmas Eve, Dick. Christmas, Ebenezer. Let's have the shutters up," he cried,

skipping down from the high desk. "Clear away, my lads, and let's have lots of room here. Hilli-ho, Dick! Chirrup, Ebenezer!"

Clear away! It was done in a minute. Then in came a fiddler with a music book. In came Mrs. Fezziwig, one vast substantial smile. In came the three Miss Fezziwigs, beaming and lovable. In came all the young men and women employed in the business. In they all came, one after another; some shyly, some boldly, some gracefully, some awkwardly, some pushing, some pulling; in they all came, anyhow and everyhow.

There were dances, and more dances, and there was cake, and mince pies. But the great effect of the evening came when old Fezziwig stood out to dance with Mrs. Fezziwig, and they were joined by three or four and twenty pair of partners.

When the clock struck eleven, this domestic ball broke up. During the whole of this time, Scrooge had acted like a man out of his wits. His heart and soul were in the scene. He remembered everything and enjoyed everything. It was not until now that he recalled the Ghost, and became conscious that it was looking full upon him.

"A small matter," said the Ghost, "to make these folks so happy."

"It isn't that," said Scrooge. "It isn't that, Spirit. He has the power to render us happy or unhappy; to make our service a pleasure or a toil. The happiness he gives is quite as great as if it cost a fortune."

He felt the Spirit's glance and stopped.

"What is the matter?" asked the Ghost.

"Nothing in particular," said Scrooge. "I should like to be able to say a word to my clerk just now. That's all."

His former self turned down the lamps, and Scrooge and the Ghost again stood side by side in the open air.

"My time grows short," observed the Spirit. "Quick!"

Again Scrooge saw himself. He was older now, a man in the prime of life. His face had not the harsh and rigid lines of later years; but it had begun to wear the signs of care and avarice. He was not alone, but sat by the side of a fair girl in whose eyes there were tears.

"It matters little," she said, softly. "To you, very little. Another idol has displaced me."

"What idol has displaced you?" he rejoined.

"A golden one. I have seen your nobler aspirations fall off one by one, until the master passion, Gain, engrosses you."

"Even so," he retorted, "I am not changed toward you."

She shook her head. "Our contract is an old one, made when we were both poor. You *are* changed. If this had never been between us," said the girl, looking steadily upon him, "tell me, would you seek me out and try to win me now?"

"You think not."

"I would gladly think otherwise if I could," she answered. "But if you were free today, can I believe that you would choose me, a dowerless girl?

I do not. And so I release you. You may have pain in this, briefly, and then you will dismiss the recollection of it as an unprofitable dream. May you be happy in the life you have chosen."

She left him, and they parted.

"Spirit!" said Scrooge. "Show me no more! Conduct me home. Why do you delight to torture me?"

"I told you these were shadows of the things that have been," said the Ghost. "That they are what they are, do not blame me!"

"Remove me!" Scrooge exclaimed. "I cannot bear it! Take me back. Haunt me no longer!"

Scrooge observed that the Spirit's light was burning high and bright. He seized the extinguisher cap and pressed it down upon the Spirit's head. The Spirit dropped beneath it, so that the extinguisher covered its whole form; but though Scrooge pressed it down with all his force, he could not hide the light.

He was conscious of being exhausted, and, further, of being in his own bedroom. He gave the cap a parting squeeze before he sank into a heavy sleep.

THE SECOND OF THE THREE SPIRITS

Scrooge awoke in the middle of a great snore and bolted up in bed. It was just before the stroke of ONE. He pushed his bed curtains aside and established a sharp lookout. Five minutes, ten minutes, a quarter of an hour went by. All this time, he lay upon his bed in a blaze of ruddy light coming from the room beyond. At last he got up to investigate and shuffled to the door.

The moment Scrooge's hand was on the lock, a strange voice bade him enter. He obeyed.

It was his own room. There was no doubt about that. But it had undergone a surprising transformation. The walls and ceiling were hung with crisp leaves of holly, mistletoe, and ivy. There were turkeys, geese, long wreaths of sausages, mince pies, plum puddings, red-hot chestnuts, cherry-cheeked apples, juicy oranges, luscious pears, and seething bowls of punch. And in easy state upon a throne, there sat a jolly Giant.

"Come in!" exclaimed the Ghost, holding his glowing torch aloft. "Come in, and know me better, man."

Scrooge entered timidly and hung his head before this Spirit.

"I am the Ghost of Christmas Present. Look upon me."

Scrooge reverently did so.

"You have never seen the like of me before!" exclaimed the Spirit.

"Never," Scrooge answered. "Spirit, conduct me where you will. I went forth before on compulsion, and I learned a lesson which is working now. This time, if you will teach me, let me profit by it."

The Ghost of Christmas Present rose. "Touch my robe."

Scrooge did as he was told.

Holly, mistletoe, berries, ivy, turkeys, geese, pies, puddings, fruit, and punch all vanished instantly. So did the room, the fire, the hour of night.

They stood in the city streets on Christmas morning, where people were scraping the snow from the pavement. There was nothing very cheerful in the climate or the town, and yet the people shoveling away were jovial and full of glee.

Soon the steeples called good people all to church and chapel, and away they came, flocking through the streets in their best clothes. And at the same time there emerged, from scores of lanes and nameless turnings, innumerable people, carrying their dinners to the bakers' shops.

Scrooge and the second Spirit went on, invisible, straight to Scrooge's clerk's. On the threshold the Spirit smiled and stopped to bless Bob Cratchit's dwelling. Think of that! Bob had very little money, and yet the Ghost of Christmas Present blessed his four-roomed house!

Up rose Mrs. Cratchit, dressed in a shabby gown, but brave in ribbons. She laid the cloth, assisted by Belinda Cratchit, while Master Peter Cratchit plunged a fork into the saucepan of potatoes. "What has ever got your precious father then?" said Mrs. Cratchit.

And now two smaller Cratchits, boy and girl, came in, and glanced out the window. "Father's coming!" they cried.

In came Bob with Tiny Tim upon his shoulder. He had been Tim's thoroughbred all the way from church. Alas for Tiny Tim, he bore a

little crutch, and had his limbs supported by an iron frame!

"Here you are at last," said Mrs. Cratchit. "And how did little Tim behave?"

"As good as gold," said Bob. "Somehow he gets thoughtful, sitting by himself so much. He told me, coming home, that he hoped the people saw him in the church, because he was a cripple, and it might be pleasant to them to remember, upon Christmas Day, who made lame beggars walk and blind men see."

Bob's voice trembled when he told them this, and trembled more when he said that Tiny Tim was growing strong and hearty.

Mrs. Cratchit made the gravy hissing hot while Master Peter mashed the potatoes and the two young Cratchits set chairs for everybody. At last the dishes were set on, grace was said, and dinner was served.

There never was such a goose. Its tenderness and flavor, size and cheapness, were the themes of universal admiration. Eked out by applesauce and mashed potatoes, it was a sufficient meal for the whole family.

Afterward, Mrs. Cratchit left the room for half a minute. She returned—flushed, but smiling proudly—with the pudding, like a speckled cannonball, blazing in brandy, and sporting Christmas holly stuck into the top.

"Oh, a wonderful pudding!" Bob Cratchit said. He

32

regarded it as the greatest success achieved by Mrs. Cratchit since their marriage. Everybody had something to say, but nobody said or thought it was at all a small pudding for a large family. Any Cratchit would have blushed to hint at such a thing.

At last the dinner was all done, the cloth was cleared, the hearth swept, and the fire made up. Apples and oranges were put upon the table, and a shovelful of chestnuts on the fire. Then all the Cratchit family drew round the hearth.

"A Merry Christmas to us all, my dears," said Bob. "God bless us!" Which all the family reechoed.

"God bless us every one!" said Tiny Tim, the last of all.

"Spirit," said Scrooge, with an interest he had never felt before, "tell me if Tiny Tim will live."

"I see a vacant seat," replied the Ghost, "and a crutch without an owner, carefully preserved. If these shadows remain, the child will die."

"No, no," said Scrooge. "Oh, no, kind Spirit. Say he will be spared."

"If these shadows remain unaltered by the Future," returned the Ghost, "none other of my race will find him here. What then? If he be like to die, he had better do it, and decrease the surplus population."

Scrooge hung his head to hear his own words quoted by the Spirit. Trembling, he cast his eyes upon the ground. But he raised them speedily on hearing his own name.

"Mr. Scrooge!" said Bob. "I give you Mr. Scrooge, the Founder of the Feast!"

"The Founder of the Feast indeed!" cried Mrs. Cratchit, reddening. "I wish I had him here. I'd give him a piece of my mind to feast upon."

"My dear," said Bob, "the children. Christmas Day."

"I'll drink his health for your sake and the Day's," said Mrs. Cratchit, "not for his. Long life to him. A Merry Christmas and A Happy New Year!"

The children drank the toast after her. It was the first of their proceedings which had no heartiness. Scrooge was the Ogre of the family. The mention of his name cast a dark shadow on the party, which was not dispelled for full five minutes. After it had passed away, they were ten times merrier than before. They were happy, grateful, and contented; and when they faded, and looked happier yet, Scrooge had his eye upon them, and especially on Tiny Tim, until the last.

By this time it was getting dark and snowing heavily. As Scrooge and the Spirit went along the streets, the brightness of the roaring fires in kitchens, parlors, and all sorts of rooms was wonderful. It was a great surprise, though, to Scrooge that he suddenly heard a hearty and familiar laugh. He recognized it as his own nephew's and at the same time found himself in a bright, gleaming room.

"Ha, ha!" laughed Scrooge's nephew. "Ha, ha, ha!"

When Scrooge's nephew laughed in this way—holding his sides, rolling his head, and twisting his face into the most extravagant contortions—Scrooge's niece by marriage laughed heartily, too, and their assembled friends roared out lustily.

"He said that Christmas was a humbug!" cried Scrooge's nephew. "He believed it, too."

"More shame for him, Fred," said Scrooge's niece indignantly.

"He's a comical old fellow," said Scrooge's nephew, "and not so pleasant as he might be. However, his offenses carry their own punishment, and I have nothing to say against him."

"I'm sure he is very rich, Fred," hinted Scrooge's niece. "At least you always tell *me* so."

"What of that, my dear!" said Scrooge's nephew. "His wealth is of no use to him. He doesn't do any good with it. He doesn't make himself comfortable with it. I am sorry for him; I couldn't be angry with him if I tried. Therefore I mean to give him the same chance every year, whether he likes it or not."

After tea Scrooge's niece played upon the harp; played among other tunes a simple little air. When this strain of music sounded, all the things that the Ghost of Christmas Past had shown Scrooge came upon his mind; and he softened more and more.

But they didn't devote the whole evening to music. There first was a game at blindman's buff. Then everyone joined in the game of How,

When, and Where. There might have been twenty people there, young and old, but they all played, and so did Scrooge. Forgetting that his voice made no sound in their ears, he sometimes came out with his guess quite loud, and very often guessed quite right, too.

There followed a game called Yes and No, where Scrooge's nephew had to think of something, and the rest must find out what, he only answering to their questions yes or no, as the case was. Under brisk questioning he revealed that he was thinking of an animal, a live animal, rather a disagreeable animal, a savage animal, an animal that growled and grunted sometimes, and talked sometimes, and lived in London, and walked about the streets, and was not a horse, or a cow, or a bull, or a dog, or a pig, or a cat, or a bear.

At every fresh question, this nephew burst into a fresh roar of laughter. At last his wife's sister, falling into a similar state, cried out:

"I know what it is, Fred! I know what it is!"

"What is it?" cried Fred.

"It's your uncle Scro-o-o-o-oge!"

Which it certainly was.

"He has given us plenty of merriment, I am sure," said Fred, "and it would be ungrateful not to drink his health. And so I say, 'Uncle Scrooge!'"

"Uncle Scrooge!" they cried.

Uncle Scrooge had become so light of heart that he would

have pledged the company in return. But the whole scene passed off in the breath of the last word spoken by his nephew, and he and the Spirit were again upon their travels.

Much they saw, and far they went, and many homes they visited, but always with a happy end. The Spirit stood beside sickbeds, and they were cheerful. In almshouse, hospital, and jail, in misery's every refuge, he left his blessing.

It was a long night, but it was strange, too, that while Scrooge remained unaltered in his outward form, the Ghost grew older, clearly older.

"Are spirits' lives so short?" asked Scrooge.

"My life upon this globe is very brief," replied the Ghost. "It ends tonight. The time is drawing near."

"Forgive me," said Scrooge, looking intently at the Spirit's robe, "but I see something strange protruding from your skirts."

"Look here," was the Spirit's sorrowful reply.

From the folds of its robe, it brought two children—wretched, abject, miserable. They were a boy and a girl. Where graceful youth should have filled their features out, a stale and shriveled hand had pinched and twisted them.

Scrooge started back, appalled. "Spirit, are they yours?"

"They are Man's," said the Spirit, looking down upon them. "This boy is Ignorance. This girl is Want."

"Have they no refuge or resource?" cried Scrooge.

"Are there no prisons?" said the Spirit, turning on him for the last time with his own words. "Are there no workhouses?"

The bell struck.

Scrooge looked about him for the Ghost and saw it not. As the last stroke ceased, he beheld a solemn Phantom, draped and hooded, coming, like a mist along the ground, toward him.

THE LAST OF THE SPIRITS

T he Phantom slowly and silently approached. It was shrouded in a deep black garment, which concealed its head, its face, its form, and left visible only its hands.

"I am in the presence of the Ghost of Christmas Yet To Come?" said Scrooge.

The Spirit answered not.

"You are about to show me shadows of the things that will happen in the time before us. Is that so, Spirit?"

The upper portion of the garment was contracted for an instant, as if the Spirit had inclined its head.

Although well used to ghostly company by this time, Scrooge trembled. "Ghost of the Future!" he exclaimed. "I fear you more than any other specter. But I know your purpose is to do me good. Will you not speak?"

It gave him no reply.

"Lead on!" said Scrooge. "The night is waning fast, and it is precious time to me, I know."

The Phantom moved away as it had come, and Scrooge followed in the shadow of its dress. They scarcely seemed to enter the city; the city rather seemed to spring up about them. But there they were, amongst the merchants, who hurried up and down, chinking the money in their pockets.

The Spirit stopped beside one little knot of businessmen. Observing that its hand was pointed to them, Scrooge advanced to listen to their talk.

"No," said a great fat man with a monstrous chin, "I don't know much about it, either. I only know he's dead."

"When did he die?" inquired another.

"Last night, I believe."

"What has he done with his money?" asked a red-faced gentleman.

"I haven't heard," said the first man, yawning. "He hasn't left it to *me*. That's all I know."

The Spirit and Scrooge left the busy scene and went into an obscure part of the town. The ways were foul and narrow; the shops and houses wretched. Scrooge and the Phantom entered one low-browed shop just as a charwoman with a heavy bundle slunk in as well. But she had scarcely entered when a laundress,

42

similarly laden, came in too, closely followed by a man in faded black. After a short period of blank astonishment, they all three burst into a laugh, for they had come from the same place.

The man in black untied his bundle first. It held a seal or two, a pencil case, a pair of sleeve buttons, and a brooch of no great value. They were examined and appraised by old Joe, the owner of the shop, who chalked the sums he was disposed to give for each upon the wall.

"That's your account," said Joe, "and I wouldn't give another sixpence, if I was to be boiled for not doing it. Who's next?"

The laundress put out sheets and towels, two old-fashioned silver teaspoons, a pair of sugar tongs, and a few boots. Her account was stated on the wall in the same manner.

"And now undo *my* bundle, Joe," said the charwoman.

Joe went down on his knees for the greater convenience of opening it, and dragged out a large and heavy roll of some dark stuff.

"What do you call this?" said Joe. "Bed curtains! You don't mean to say you took them down, rings and all, with him lying there?"

"Why not?" replied the woman. "If he wanted to keep them after he was dead, he'd have had somebody to look after him, instead of gasping out his last there, alone by himself. You may look through that shirt till your eyes ache; but you won't find a hole in it. It's the best he had, and a fine one too. They'd have wasted it, if it hadn't been for me."

"What do you call wasting it?" asked old Joe.

"Putting it on him to be buried in. Somebody was fool enough to do it, but I took it off again."

Scrooge listened to this dialogue in horror. "Spirit," he said, shuddering from head to foot. "I see, I see. The case of this unhappy man might be my own. My life tends that way now. Merciful Heaven, what is this!"

He recoiled in terror, for the scene had changed. Now he stood by a bare, uncurtained bed, on which, beneath a ragged sheet, there lay something covered up.

The room was very dark. A pale light, rising in the outer air, fell straight upon the bed; and on it, unwatched and uncared for, was the body of this man.

Scrooge glanced toward the Phantom. Its steady hand was pointed to the head. The cover was so carelessly adjusted that the slightest raising of it would have disclosed the face.

"I understand you," said Scrooge, "and I would do it, if I could. But I have not the power, Spirit."

Again it seemed to look upon him. Then the Ghost conducted him through several streets familiar to his feet. They entered poor Bob Cratchit's house, and found his family seated round the fire.

Quiet. Very quiet. The noisy little Cratchits were as still as statues. The mother and her daughters were engaged in sewing.

"It must be near your father's time," said Mrs. Cratchit.

"Past it rather," Peter answered, shutting up his book. "But I think he has walked a little slower than he used to, Mother."

They were very quiet again. At last Mrs. Cratchit said, and in a steady, cheerful voice, that only faltered once: "I have known him walk with—I have known him walk with Tiny Tim upon his shoulder, very fast indeed."

"And so have I," cried Peter. "Often."

"And so have I," exclaimed another. So had all.

"But he was very light to carry," she resumed, "and your father loved him so, that it was no trouble—no trouble. And there is your father at the door!"

She hurried out to meet him.

"You went today, then, Robert?" said Mrs. Cratchit.

"Yes, my dear," returned Bob. "I wish you could have gone. It would have done you good to see how green a place it is. I promised him that I would walk there on a Sunday. My little, little child! My little child!"

He broke down all at once. He couldn't help it. Then they all drew about the fire, and talked, the girls and mother working still.

"Specter," said Scrooge, "something informs me that our parting moment is at hand. I know it, but I know not how. Tell me what man that was whom we saw lying dead."

The Ghost of Christmas Yet To Come conveyed him to an iron gate. He paused to look round before entering.

A churchyard. Here, then, the wretched man, whose name he had now to learn, lay underneath the ground. The Spirit stood among the graves and pointed down to one.

Scrooge advanced toward it trembling. "Answer me one question," he said. "Are these the shadows of the things that Will be, or are they shadows of things that May be, only?"

Still the Ghost pointed downward to the grave.

"Men's courses foreshadow certain ends," said Scrooge. "But if the courses be departed from, the ends will change. Is this not true?"

The Spirit was immovable as ever.

Scrooge crept toward it, trembling as he went, and, following the finger, read upon the stone his own name, EBENEZER SCROOGE.

"Am *I* that man who lay upon the bed?" he cried, upon his knees.

The finger pointed from the grave to him, and back again.

"No, Spirit! Oh no, no!" he cried, clutching at its robe. "Hear me. I am not the man I was. Why show me this, if I am past all hope!"

For the first time the hand appeared to shake.

"Good Spirit," he pursued, "assure me that I yet may change these shadows by an altered life!"

The kind hand trembled.

"I will honor Christmas in my heart, and try to keep it all the year. I will live in the Past, the Present, and the Future. The Spirits of all Three shall strive within me."

Holding up his hands in a last prayer to have his fate reversed, Scrooge saw an alteration in the Phantom's hood and dress. It shrunk, collapsed, and dwindled down into a bedpost.

THE END OF IT

Yes! And the bedpost was his own. The bed was his own, the room was his own. Best and happiest of all, the Time before him was his own to make amends in!

"I will live in the Past, the Present, and the Future!" Scrooge repeated. "The Spirits of all Three shall strive within me. I say it on my knees, old Jacob, on my knees!"

He was fluttered and glowing with his good intentions. "I don't know what to do!" cried Scrooge, laughing and crying in the same breath. "I am as light as a feather, I am as happy as an angel, I am as merry as a schoolboy. A Merry Christmas to everybody! A Happy New Year to all the world!"

He had frisked into the sitting room and was now standing there, perfectly winded.

"There's the door, by which the Ghost of Jacob Marley entered!" cried Scrooge. "There's the corner where the Ghost of Christmas Present sat. There's the window where I saw the wandering Spirits. It's all right, it's all true. Ha ha ha!"

Really, for a man who had been out of practice for so many years, it was a splendid laugh, a most illustrious laugh. The father of a long, long line of brilliant laughs!

"I don't know what day it is!" said Scrooge. "I don't know how long I've been among the Spirits. I don't know anything. Never mind. I don't care."

Running to the window, he opened it and put out his head. No fog, no mist—clear, bright, golden sunlight. Oh, glorious. Glorious!

"What's today?" cried Scrooge, calling downward to a boy in Sunday clothes.

"Eh?"

"What's today, my fine fellow?" said Scrooge.

"Today?" replied the boy. "Why, CHRISTMAS DAY."

"It's Christmas Day!" said Scrooge to himself. "I haven't missed it. The Spirits have done it all in one night. They can do anything they like. Of course they can. Hallo, my fine fellow!"

"Hallo!" returned the boy.

"Do you know the butcher's in the next street but one?" Scrooge inquired.

"I should hope I did," replied the lad.

"An intelligent boy!" said Scrooge. "A remarkable boy! Do you know whether they've sold the prize turkey that was hanging up there?"

"What, the one as big as me?"

"What a delightful boy!" said Scrooge. "It's a pleasure to talk to him. Yes, my buck."

"It's hanging there now."

"Is it?" said Scrooge. "Go and buy it."

"Who? Me?" exclaimed the boy.

"I am in earnest," said Scrooge. "Go and buy it,

and tell them to bring it here. Come back with the man, and I'll give you a shilling. Come back with him in less than five minutes and I'll give you half a crown."

The boy was off like a shot.

"I'll send it to Bob Cratchit's!" whispered Scrooge, rubbing his hands. "He shan't know who sends it. It's twice the size of Tiny Tim."

The hand in which he wrote the address was not a steady one, but write it he did, somehow. As he stood waiting for the butcher's man, the knocker caught his eye.

"I shall love it as long as I live!" cried Scrooge, patting it with his hand. "What an honest expression it has in its face. It's a wonderful knocker! –Here's the turkey. Hallo! How are you? Merry Christmas!"

It *was* a turkey! He never could have stood upon his legs, that bird. He would have snapped them off in a minute.

"Why, it's impossible to carry that to Camden Town," Scrooge told the butcher's man. "You must have a cab."

The chuckle with which he said this, and the chuckle with which he paid for the turkey, and the chuckle with which he paid for the cab, and the chuckle with which he recompensed the boy, were only exceeded by the chuckle with which he sat down breathless in his chair again.

He dressed himself all in his best, and at last got out into the streets. The people were by this time pouring forth, as he had seen them with the Ghost of Christmas Present.

He had not gone far when he beheld the portly gentleman who had visited him the day before and said, "Scrooge and Marley's, I believe?"

"My dear sir," said Scrooge, taking the old gentleman by both his hands. "How do you do. I hope you succeeded yesterday. A Merry Christmas to you, sir!"

"Mr. Scrooge?"

"Yes," said Scrooge. "That is my name, and I fear it may not be pleasant to you. Allow me to ask your pardon. And will you have the goodness—" Here Scrooge whispered in his ear.

"Lord bless me!" cried the gentleman. "My dear Mr. Scrooge, are you serious?"

"If you please," said Scrooge. "Not a farthing less. A great many back payments are included in it, I assure you."

"My dear sir," said the other, shaking hands with him. "I don't know what to say."

"Don't say anything, please," retorted Scrooge. "I am much obliged to you. I thank you fifty times. Bless you!"

He went to church, and walked about the streets, and watched the people hurrying to and fro, and patted children on the head. He had never dreamed that any walk—that anything—could give him so much happiness. In the afternoon he turned his steps toward his nephew's house.

He passed the door a dozen times before he had the courage to go up and knock.

"Is your master at home, my dear?" said Scrooge to the girl. Nice girl. Very.

"Yes, sir."

"Where is he, my love?" said Scrooge.

"He's in the dining room, sir, along with mistress. I'll show you upstairs, if you please."

"Thank you. He knows me," said Scrooge, with his hand already on the dining-room lock. He turned it gently and sidled his face in, round the door.

"Fred!" said Scrooge.

"Why bless my soul!" cried Fred. "Who's that?"

"It's I. Your uncle Scrooge. I have come to dinner. Will you let me in, Fred?"

Let him in! It is a mercy he didn't shake his arm off. He was at home in five minutes. Nothing could be heartier. His niece looked just the same. So did everyone when *they* came. Wonderful party, wonderful games, won-der-ful happiness!

But he was early at the office next morning. Oh, he was early there. If he could only be there first, and catch Bob Cratchit coming late! That was the thing he had set his heart upon.

And he did it. The clock struck nine. No Bob. A quarter past. No Bob. He was full eighteen minutes and a half behind his time. Scrooge sat with his door wide open, that he might see him come in.

His hat was off before he opened the door. He was on his stool in a jiffy, driving away with his pen.

"Hallo," growled Scrooge, in his accustomed voice, as near as he could feign it. "What do you mean by coming here at this time of day?"

"I'm very sorry, sir," said Bob. "I *am* behind my time."

"You are?" repeated Scrooge. "Yes. I think you are. Step this way, if you please."

"It's only once a year, sir," pleaded Bob. "It shall not be repeated. I was making rather merry yesterday, sir."

"Now, I'll tell you what, my friend," said Scrooge, "I am not going to stand this sort of thing any longer. And therefore," he continued, leaping from his stool and giving Bob a dig in the waistcoat, "and therefore I am about to raise your salary!"

Bob trembled, and got a little nearer to the ruler. He had a momentary idea of knocking Scrooge down with it and calling to the people outside for help.

"A Merry Christmas, Bob," said Scrooge, with an earnestness that could not be mistaken. "A merrier Christmas, Bob, than I have ever given you. I'll raise your salary, and endeavor to assist your struggling family. We will discuss your affairs this very afternoon, over a bowl of Christmas punch. But for now, make up the fires, and buy another coal scuttle before you dot another i, Bob Cratchit!"

Scrooge was better than his word. He did it all, and infinitely more. And to Tiny Tim, who did *not* die, he was a second father. He became as good a friend, as good a master, and as good a man as the good old city knew.

He had no further dealings with Spirits, but it was always said of him that he knew how to keep Christmas well. May that be truly said of us, and all of us! And so, as Tiny Tim observed, God Bless Us, Every One!

DEAN MORRISSEY began his painting career in the 1970s. His first children's book, *Ship of Dreams*, was a *New York Times* Best Illustrated Book of 1994. He is also the author and illustrator of *The Great Kettles*, *The Christmas Ship*, and *The Moon Robber*. Infusing the pictures with texture, color, light, and weight, Dean Morrissey creates a compelling atmosphere for his stories.

Dean Morrissey lives on the South Shore of Massachusetts with his wife and son.

STEPHEN KRENSKY is the author of over fifty books for children, including *How Santa Got His Job* (an ALA Notable Book). While he has long been an admirer of *A Christmas Carol*, he remains thankful that no ghosts have yet chosen to pay him a visit. Mr. Krensky lives in Lexington, Massachusetts, with his wife, Joan, and their two children.